the VERY WORST ever

Pop Goes the Carnival

BY ANDY NONAMUS
ILLUSTRATED BY AMY JINDRA

LITTLE SIMON

NEW YORK LONDON TORONTO SYDNEY NEW DELHI

This book is a work of fiction. Any references to historical events, real people, or real places are used fictiously. Other names, characters, places, and events are products of the author's imagination, and any resemblance to actual events or places or persons, living or dead, is entirely coincidental.

LITTLE SIMON
An imprint of Simon & Schuster Children's Publishing Division
1230 Avenue of the Americas, New York, New York 10020
First Little Simon paperback edition January 2024
Copyright © 2024 by Simon & Schuster, LLC
Also available in a Little Simon hardcover edition
All rights reserved, including the right of reproduction in whole or in part in any form.
LITTLE SIMON is a registered trademark of Simon & Schuster, LLC, and associated colophon is a trademark of Simon & Schuster, LLC.
Simon & Schuster: Celebrating 100 Years of Publishing in 2024
For information about special discounts for bulk purchases, please contact Simon & Schuster Special Sales at 1-866-506-1949 or business@simonandschuster.com.
The Simon & Schuster Speakers Bureau can bring authors to your live event. For more information or to book an event contact the Simon & Schuster Speakers Bureau at 1-866-248-3049 or visit our website at www.simonspeakers.com.
Designed by Leslie Mechanic
The text of this book was set in Causten Round.
Manufactured in the United States of America 1223 LAK
10 9 8 7 6 5 4 3 2 1
Library of Congress Cataloging in Publication Data
Names: Nonamus, Andy, author. | Jindra, Amy, illustrator. | Nonamus, Andy. First day, worst day
Title: Pop goes the carnival / by Andy Nonamus ; illustrated by Amy Jindra.
Description: First Little Simon edition. | New York : Little Simon, 2024. | Series: The very worst ever ; book 2 | Audience: Ages 5–9. | Summary: A self-proclaimed elementary-school student, who wishes to remain anonymous, tries to avoid disaster as he creates a booth for his school carnival and attempts to win a lucky bracelet.
Identifiers: LCCN 2023021695 (print) | LCCN 2023021696 (ebook) | ISBN 9781665942232 (paperback) | ISBN 9781665942249 (hardcover) | ISBN 9781665942256 (ebook)
Subjects: CYAC: Carnivals–Fiction. | Luck–Fiction. | Elementary schools–Fiction. | Schools–Fiction. | BISAC: JUVENILE FICTION / Humorous Stories | JUVENILE FICTION / Readers / Chapter Books | LCGFT:
Classification: LCC PZ7.1.N6378 Po 2024 (print) | LCC PZ7.1.N6378 (ebook) | DDC [Fic]–dc23
LC record available at https://lccn.loc.gov/2023021695
LC ebook record available at https://lccn.loc.gov/2023021696

CONTENTS

Hey, Reader!

Thanks for checking out my story.
Though I gotta warn you, I can't ever
let you know my real name or what
I look like. This may seem weird, but
trust me, it's very important that I
stay a secret.

Why? To protect myself! Seriously,
these stories are super embarrassing!

Plus, you might even know me already!
I could be in your class, on your
baseball team, in your ballet class, or
playing the tuba in your school band . . .
anywhere!

Hi!

For all you know I could be sitting next to you right now!

So I went ahead and scratched out my name and put a sticker on my face, so you don't have to. You're welcome.

Now, we can both enjoy reading all about my awkward life . . . if you're into that kind of thing.

Peace out!

CLASS CLOWN

When I say "class clown," you might think of a silly kid from school. They might even make animal noises during class. *Caw-caw*, they'd say, like a toucan. Or *ooooh-ahhh-ah-ah*, like a monkey.

Hilarious, right?

Yeah ... this wasn't like that.

I walked into classroom 312 to see a class clown . . . but it wasn't even human! It was a balloon with a red nose and a teardrop on its face. Inside the clown, tiny weights helped it always stand upright. Even if you threw your backpack at it, the clown would bounce back up with its beady little eyes.

And just my luck, it was right next to my desk.

I made my way over carefully and tried to sit down without making eye contact. But the moment I tried to scoot my desk up just a tad bit, the clown rocked down and booped the top of my head.

"AGH!" I shouted, trying to get away.

Mr. Hughes, my teacher, grinned in front of the board. "Ah, ██████████, I see you've met Happy."

"This thing's name is *Happy*?" I squeaked.

"I got you, bro!" said a voice across the classroom.

It was Jake Gold. He was best at gym class and best at being one of my new best friends. He leapt over all the desks and ever-so-gently pushed Happy away from me.

"Thanks for that save," I said.

He swished his sparkling hair. "Sure, bro. It's, like, class time. Not time to clown around."

Mr. Hughes clapped, getting everyone's attention. "Jake, would you mind heading back to your seat?"

"Yes, sir!" Jake cartwheeled back.

"Great!" said Mr. Hughes as everyone settled in. "I just want to give a friendly reminder that the school carnival is tomorrow night. You should all be working on your booths!

On the sign: PLEASE DON'T FEED FLUFFY JELLY BEANS.

No pressure, but . . . I'm expecting BIG things!"

And that was when it hit me.

(No, not Happy's nose.)

Carnival? Booths?? BIG things??!!!

I had completely forgotten about creating a booth for the school carnival! Looked like there were two clowns in this class, and one of them was me.

2

A VERY LUCKY PRIZE

Of course, every other kid in class already had their booth planned.

"I'm doing a golf booth, but with GIANT beach balls instead of golf balls," one kid bragged.

"Oh yeah? Well, at mine, you can throw darts . . . at SODA-FILLED BALLOONS!" a girl said.

As the whole class kept talking about their perfect booth ideas, I kinda zoned out. Because while a carnival seems like the coolest event of the year, I knew what it really was. An epic danger zone!

But carnivals have funnel cake, you're thinking. What could be so dangerous about a place with funnel cake?

Funnel cakes are fine. But mix in a freak windstorm and *boom!* You're covered in powdered sugar and running from a flock of birds with a major sweet tooth.

But what about *carnival rides?* you wonder.

I did like the teacups ride . . . until it spun out of control! Somehow, the ride went haywire and sent *only* my teacup into a blur.

A really messy, *barfy* blur.

And don't even get me started on what happened at the bouncy castle. Why did I wear super-pointy-tipped shoes that day?

I snapped out of my daydream just as Mr. Hughes said, "And there's a very lucky prize for the carnival's most popular booth!"

That got everyone's attention.

"No quizzes for the rest of the year?" someone gasped.

"More gym classes?" Jake shouted, practically fainting.

"Not quite . . ." Mr. Hughes turned his back like a showman and then spun around dramatically with something shiny in his hands. "It's a *LUCKY BRACELET!*"

The bracelet glinted in the sunlight.
It had a gold chain and a sparkling
four-leaf-clover charm. And invisible
to the human eye, it had one hundred
percent real luck all over it.

My future flashed before my eyes. No more spilled drinks, no more raccoons chasing me, no more *anything* getting stuck on my shoes.

This bracelet could change everything.

I *had* to win it.

3

BEWARE THE TETHERBALL

To win that lucky bracelet, I'd need to think up the wildest carnival booth this school had ever seen. And at a place like this school, that wouldn't be easy. Our gym was a library. Some of our teachers were mimes. Recently, the school bells stopped ringing and started *mooing*.

This school was weird. If I wanted to stand out at the carnival, I'd have to think *way* outside the box.

Good thing I was already standing outside.

MOOOOOOOOOOO!!!

That "moo" meant it was lunchtime. Normally, you'd do this inside—you know, in a cafeteria. Well, not here.

New-School's cafeteria was outside, ON THE PLAYGROUND. The lunch tables were in between seesaws and jungle gyms. If you wanted to eat with your friends, you'd better dodge the kickball game and avoid the tetherball stand.

Trust me, you do *not* want to have lunch next to the tetherball stand.

One time, a kid named Stan Dup sat too close to the tetherball stand. It knocked him right into the sky. He has not been seen since.

"Hot lunch?" the cafeteria lady asked, headbutting a soccer ball away from the food.

I nodded and grabbed my tray of mystery mush, sprinting to my table before the Frisbees started flying. Jake and my other new friend, Regina du Lar, were already there.

"Where's Glinda?" I asked.

Before anyone could reply, a dark cloud loomed above. "You rang?"

I looked up to see a very short, very spooky goth girl at the top of a slide near our table. She slid down toward us but never once looked happy about it. This was Glinda Alegre.

"Good to see you getting some sun," I joked.

"You know me," she said, deadpan. "Just soaking up all the vitamin D . . . until the sun has none left . . . and completely disappears."

Jake's eyes widened. "Is that possible?"

"The sun isn't going anywhere," Regina said. "But my carnival booth is definitely going places! Check it out."

Regina pulled out her tablet, and we all ducked as a kickball sailed over our table.

"Wait," I said. "You're building a booth too? But you're not in our class."

"Every student builds a booth," Glinda said.

I gulped hard. "The *whole* school's competing for the lucky bracelet?"

"Duh!" Regina smiled. "In my video game booth, you can BECOME the characters."

Jake flexed. "Mine's an extreme gym! With extra-sweaty towels!"

We all looked to Glinda, who stayed
quiet for a moment. "My booth is
a secret. A dark . . . none-of-your-
business . . . secret."

"What's yours?" Jake asked me.

"Mine is . . . a secret too," I said.

Glinda smiled, which made me break into a cold sweat. It was like when dinosaurs smile at tiny kids in movies. "That means he hasn't started yet . . . and the carnival's tomorrow night."

The clock was ticking . . .

And the school bell was *mooing*.

4

A CHANCE OF NIGHTMARES

That night, I planned to stay up late to work on my Big Booth Idea. But my eyelids failed me. As soon as Mom hit the lights, my all-nighter brainstorm turned into more of a sleep-nado.

Forecast: one hundred percent chance of nightmares!

Sometimes, nightmares were silly.

I'd fought space aliens and goopy monsters in my dreams before. But this . . . this was *much* worse.

One by one, I had visions of my friends at the carnival in their booths . . . WHICH WERE BETTER THAN MINE!

Dun-dun-duuuun!

First up was Regina's. It was a virtual reality party, where glitter fell like snow. Through the sparkles, I saw her singing onstage with a band made up of cute animals. There was even a DJ made of pixels and a singing goblin warrior.

My dream suddenly transported me to Jake's booth. It was a Nightmare Gym! The entire floor was a treadmill. I tried to escape, but two bodybuilders stood in my way. When I looked up, they both had Jake's face!

"Hey, dude! Wanna drop and give us A MILLION PUSH-UPS?" the Jake Clones asked in his friendly way.

When I couldn't even do one, they grabbed a fire hose.

"That's okay," I squeaked. "I'm not thirsty."

"It's not water," they roared. "It's SWEAT!"

KER-SPLAAASH!

The fire hose drenched me in someone else's mystery sweat. Some of it got in my mouth. Gross!

Then, everything went black.

"That's right," a familiar voice echoed from the darkness. "You can't even imagine my booth in your dreams . . . that's how secret it is! Mwah-ha-HAAAAH!"

I recognized that evil laugh. It was Glinda!

Could this nightmare get any worse?

Oh, it could. Because out of the shadows floated the last face I wanted to see in the dark.

It was Happy the Sad Clown!

"Where's your booth, ▓▓▓▓▓▓?" he asked.

"I don't know!" I shouted.

"But don't you want to win?" He frowned. "Don't you want your luck to change?"

He pulled out a bike horn from his pocket and chased me with it. Not only did I hear the horn, but I saw the actual sounds spelled out in floating words!

BEEP! BEEP!

The words separated into single letters, and then the letters swirled around me! The echoing became louder and louder.

BEEP! BEEP! BEEP!

"I DO WANT TO WIN!" I shouted, springing awake. Realizing I was in my bedroom, I sighed a breath of relief. I was even grateful to be drenched in my *own* sweat.

There was no way I could lose this lucky bracelet. I grabbed a pen and paper. My brain shot out ideas faster than my hand could scribble them. Before I knew it, the birds were chirping, the sun blazed into my room, and my booth design was sketched out.

"It's *alive!*" I screamed.

IT'S

ALIVE!

5

BANANA PEELS AND DREAM BUILDS

Despite running in slow motion, I somehow made it to school before the first bell. I ran even faster down the hallway to classroom 312. I was moving so fast, I completely missed the sign that read WET FLOOR—BANANA PEELS AHEAD.

Wait—banana peels?!

"Onwaaaaaard!" I screamed.

I slid on one of the peels and right into Mr. Hughes's desk.

He had been grading papers and jumped in surprise. "Whoa! Didn't you read the sign out there? It was very clear."

I tossed the peel into the trash can. "Where did those peels even come from?"

Mr. Hughes pointed to a poster on the door. It read JOIN THE BANANA CLUB! WE ARE ALWAYS A-PEELING!

"Oh, that's from the Banana Club meeting this morning," he said. "I really regret starting it. The peels wind up everywhere!"

I frowned. "The Banana Club? You're joking, right?"

"I *never* joke about the Banana Club," Mr. Hughes said. "That would be *bananas*. What brings you to class so early?"

It was finally my time to shine. "I have something I want to show you. It's . . . my booth idea!"

I slammed my drawing down on his desk. He picked it up and hummed thoughtfully, turning the sketch this way and that.

"Behold . . . a GIANT CLAW MACHINE!" I announced proudly.

"It's incredible, ████████, but . . . how will you build this in time?" Mr. Hughes asked.

I shrugged in what I hoped was a cool way. "I know a gal."

(By "gal," I meant Mom.)

Over the years, Mom had held tons of random jobs. From ice sculptor to choir teacher to stuntperson, she knew how to make things happen. At this new construction job, she was building things all day! If anyone could help me, it was her.

I slid Mr. Hughes her business card.

"'Dream Builders Construction,'" Mr. Hughes read aloud. "'You dream it, we build it.' Whoa—this could be a winner if it's done right."

That was just the confidence boost I needed. Things were looking up as I made my way to my desk. I hopped over a banana peel. All was well in classroom 312. Even Happy the Sad Clown was gone. At least, I thought he was gone. You know what they say about clown balloons: they are full of hot air, but they can bring the hot scare.

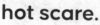

6

BEWARE, DISASTER!

Finally, the sun set and it was time for the carnival. How could I tell? Because everything looked red and white.

(No, I didn't suddenly have candy-cane vision.)

Our school parking lot had been transformed into a maze of peppermint-striped booths.

Twinkling lights looped over the tops. A Ferris wheel loomed over the horizon, and the smell of sweets made my mouth start to water. There was even a stage with a bunch of dads playingelectricguitarsforsomereason. It looked like the whole neighborhood had shown up this evening.

The school carnival was officially open!

I found where my booth should be, but there was nothing there. Just a sad plot of land covered in cement. But I knew Mom would show up. In fact, I could hear her now, saying, "Watch out, sweetie pie!"

Wait . . . that really *was* her!

I looked up, and she was in a helicopter right above me! Next to her, the pilot slowly lowered a giant item wrapped in cloth. It was so big, it almost looked like they were secretly carrying a giraffe around!

BEEP! BEEP! BEEP!

"Is that what I think it is?!" I shouted over the noise.

"Let's find out!" Mom shouted. A rope dropped, and she swung down to meet me. The pilot released the giant cloth-wrapped item, and we waved as he flew off.

Mom grabbed the string tied around the cloth. "Ready? One . . . two . . . THREE!"

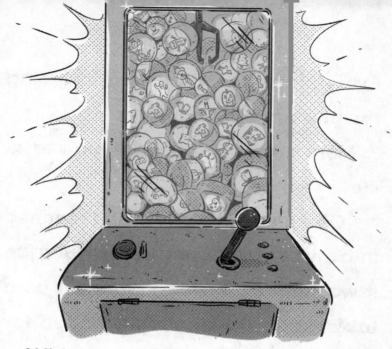

With one swift tug, the cloth fell
and a giant booth stood before me. A
built-in claw machine was there too,
larger than life and filled with prizes.
Prizes that were going to win me that
lucky bracelet.

"MY CLAW MACHINE!" I gasped.

Everything about it was big, including the mystery prize capsules inside.

Mom turned it on and it glowed to life.

"Oh, I almost forgot this!" I reached into my backpack and pulled out a jar. It was labeled VOTES. I placed it on a table, sat on a stool, and waited for kids to line up.

And waited.

And waited.

And waited.

I sprang up from my seat. "Why is it taking so long to win votes?!"

"Why don't you catch up with your friends and enjoy the carnival?" Mom suggested. "I can keep an eye on things."

"Okay . . . ," I said, trying to feel calmer. If there was anyone I trusted with my booth, it was Mom. I mean, she *had* broken every toaster we'd ever owned, but she always had my back. What could go wrong?

"YES," I heard a familiar voice echo. "WHAT *COULD* GO WRONG? . . .

. . . *WRONG* . . .

. . . . . . *wrong* . . . . . .

. . . . *w . . . r . . . o . . . n . . . g . . . .*"

The echo was coming from a strange booth next door. I stepped out to see a black tent with eyes painted on it. The sign over it read GLINDA SEES ALL.

I entered and saw Glinda sitting in the dark with a crystal ball.

"Um, were you reading my mind just now?" I asked.

"Maybe I was," she said in a strange fortune-teller voice. "Why don't you sit down and let me read your future? I promise, it's quite terrible."

"Sure." I sat down. I knew Glinda liked terrible things.

She waved her hands over the crystal ball and smiled. It was freaking me out.

"Beware," she warned. "I see disaster in your future. Terrible, unlucky disaster!"

"That sounds like a normal day for me," I said.

Her smile became even creepier. "But what I *don't* see ... is that bracelet you're after."

"Wait—WHAT?" I cried out.

"I see . . . an ugly blanket!" Glinda said. "There!"

A kid had just walked into the tent holding a very familiar, very ugly blanket with a parrot on it. He froze as we stared at him.

"That's strange," I said. "That looks like the blanket Granny knit for me. She loves parrots."

"I got it from the giant claw machine next door," the kid said. "It's giving out all kinds of weird free stuff."

"Told you," Glinda said smugly. "Disaster."

Oh no.

7

PRIZES AND CLOWNS

I rushed out of the tent and right into the worst scene I'd ever seen. Kids walked around with all sorts of random stuff. My random stuff. I saw *my* alien shower cap, *my* monster trading cards, and even *my* piggy bank.

"Not Mr. Oinky!" I cried. "That has my life savings! All thirteen dollars!"

The longest line I had ever seen wrapped around the booths. Can you guess what everyone was waiting for? That's right—a chance to use the giant claw machine.

I watched as someone won my diary, then my baby teeth. Mr. Bookman, our school librarian, won

my old retainer. It was embarrassing.

"Mom!" I huffed and puffed back to my booth. "Did you put MY stuff in the claw machine?"

"Of course!" Mom said. "It's YOUR machine. Shouldn't it have YOUR stuff in it? Now, how about some funnel cake? I'll be right back!"

Before I could say another word, Mom was gone. Nothing gets between her and a funnel cake.

A girl tapped on my shoulder and held up my toothbrush. "Can I get some toothpaste to go with this? Seems like an incomplete prize."

I snatched it back from her. "Kids can't share toothbrushes! Think about all the germs."

The girl rolled her eyes and got back in line.

I was about to shut the machine down, when a voice said, "Look at this crowd!"

It was hard to see him underneath the ogre makeup and giant party glasses, but I was *pretty* sure I was talking to Mr. Hughes.

"Is that stuff from Regina's video game party booth?" I asked.

"Of course!" he replied. "I don't . . . *ahem* . . . own this costume." He quickly changed the subject. "Hey, look at those votes!"

(GASP! I had totally forgotten about the votes!)

A glimmer of hope suddenly shone through my booth...and it was coming from the votes jar. It was stuffed with tickets! Hundreds—no, *thousands!*

Mr. Hughes high-fived me. "I think that lucky bracelet could be yours. Happy the Sad Clown sure looks proud of you! Nice of you to let him hang out here."

A knot immediately formed in my throat. "H-Happy?"

Slowly, I turned. Time seemed to stop as a chill ran up my spine.

There, in the corner of my booth, I saw a face lean forward from out of the shadows. The red nose. The teary-eyed face. The creepiness.

"AAAAAGH!!!" I shrieked. "How'd
you get in here?!"

I tumbled back in fright, bumping
right into the claw machine. My elbows
hit all the buttons at once, setting off
alarm sirens.

Smoke rose from inside of the machine, making gears and sparks fly out. Everyone gasped and moved out of the way.

All I could do was watch the claw machine tip over, releasing all the capsules inside. It was a full-on...

8

AVALANCHES AND
ROLLER COASTERS

...PRIZE AVALANCHE!

Did you know avalanches can be surfed just like a wave? Sadly, I wasn't a surfer. I was just a very unlucky kid. That's why the Prize Avalanche knocked me clean off my feet and washed me away like a rag doll.

"MOOOOOVE!" I screamed.

I waved my arms around, trying to warn the crowd. There just wasn't enough time. People standing in line for hot pretzels were suddenly twisted up under a rushing wave of my stuff.

My secret plushie collection, my used Halloween costumes, my old train set. Who knew how much stuff I had in my closet? The Prize Avalanche swallowed up a candy stand, threw the ring-toss booth around, and even spun the Ferris wheel!

I bobbed up for air and saw a big boulder ahead. It split the avalanche down the middle. It sliced through the capsules as if they were water!

That was when I saw the swish of hair.

"████████!" Jake shouted. "I've got you!"

As I rushed closer, I noticed he was holding up something round. It was a sticky candy apple!

"I'm not really hungry!" I yelled.

"Grab it and I'll pull you out!" he shouted.

Whoa—that was actually a good idea.

As I got closer, I reached out my arm and waited...waited...and completely missed it. Instead of holding on to the candy apple with my hand, it got stuck in my hair and pulled Jake in!

"Are you okay?!" I tried to balance myself on a rolling capsule.

"Dude!" Jake shouted. "Your hair took my snack! What am I supposed to eat now?" Then he brightened. "Oh, look! I'll just eat that."

I turned to look. Sure enough, there was the kettle corn machine. Only this was no normal popper. Karla's Kettle Corn stand was known for being absolutely massive. It whirred and popped and crackled kettle corn.

And we were on a collision course, headed straight for it.

SCREEEEEEEEEECH!

As if it didn't want to be caught up in popcorn, the Prize Avalanche tried to stop itself before it slammed into the kettle corn machine.

It dumped us out, and then the flood of my things disappeared down another path.

"Ugh," I groaned, thinking of the mess I'd caused. "This is going to be worse than cleaning my room."

"Yum! This thing is—*crunch*—amazing!" Jake said. He was popping tons of popcorn into his mouth all at once.

I looked around and realized we were inside the kettle corn machine popper. Popcorn popped and bounced all around us.

"Um, Jake, we need to get out of here," I said.

But there was no talking sense into my friend. He said, "Bro, there's no way I'm leaving."

We saw the glowing red button at the same time. It was labeled FASTER.

"Hey, look! This ride has a 'faster' option!" Jake said.

"This isn't a ride!" I shouted.

Guess what happened next? Jake smashed the button. The kernels began to pop faster and louder. Before I knew it, there was so much kettle corn, the machine was overflowing.

CREEEEAK! We started to tip over.

"IT'S GONNA POP!" a kid shouted.

And you know what? It *did* pop. The kettle corn burst out of the machine like a giant wave. No, not a wave—a roller coaster. And we were riding on it through the entire carnival.

9

A POPPIN' TIME

The Kettle Corn Roller Coaster took everything in its path. Kids, the guitar-playing dads, and even Happy the Sad Clown. He popped out beside me, and I quickly shoved him back into the popcorn wave.

We went up, down, sideways, and over through the booths.

Jake suddenly appeared, dog-paddling his way forward as Glinda sat on his back.

"Is there something on my back?" Jake shouted.

I frowned at Glinda. "When did you get here?!"

"Your wave destroyed my booth," she said, then smiled eerily. "It was amazing."

This was definitely the disaster she had seen in her crystal ball. There was no way I was winning that lucky bracelet now.

Just when I thought we were done for, I heard a familiar voice shouting, " ██████ , GLINDA, JAKE!"

With all the kettle corn flying around, I barely spotted Regina a few feet ahead of us.

"Run while you can!" I screamed.

"Looks like you could use a claw!" she shouted back.

Huh? I tried to get a better look. Regina ran to my claw machine and took control of it. Everyone watched in awe as she used the claw to pick up the huge cloth it had been delivered in.

"Steady ... steady ... ," she shouted.
Just as we passed by, Regina
scooped us up with the giant bag!

Glinda, Jake, and I popped to the
very top of the popcorn bag.

It felt like a million eyes suddenly turned to look at me. I squeezed mine shut, waiting for them to start shouting angrily.

They're going to think I'm the worst ever, I thought.

But to my surprise, everyone started cheering and clapping! My eyes snapped open.

"THAT . . . WAS . . . AMAZING!" Jake shouted. He dove in and out of the popcorn, like a dolphin.

"Total chaos," Glinda said. Then she mysteriously sank into the bag.

"That was a poppin' time!" one of the guitar dads added.

I couldn't believe what I was hearing. "Are you guys saying . . . you liked this?"

"BEST CARNIVAL EVER!" someone shouted. "Your ride gets ALL my votes!"

Then everyone started chanting my name. "████████! ████████! ████████!"

And it wasn't even in a bad way!

10

THE MEANING OF LUCK

For someone who ran a booth with a giant claw, it turned out I wasn't very good at using it.

Thankfully, Regina was great at it.

Along with Jake and Glinda, she stuck around long after everyone had gone home. Good friends have fun with you at a carnival.

But best friends, well, they help you clean up your mess.

With a button push here and a joystick swivel there, I watched as she picked up popcorn and dumped it into the dumpster.

Glinda pretended not to help, but she kicked a few bits behind a bush. It wasn't exactly the trash can, but some squirrels were having the best dinner ever.

Jake helped by tossing kernels into the trash like basketballs. "SLAM DUNK! TOUCHDOWN! Uh...GOAL!"

As I scooped up the last scraps of trash, Mr. Hughes found me at the claw machine. "You forgot something."

I watched in disbelief as he tossed something shiny to me. I stuck my hand out in the wrong direction, but I still caught it. This could only mean one thing. . . .

It was the lucky bracelet! Its four-leaf-clover charm sparkled in the palm of my hand.

"I tallied up the votes, and you WON Most Popular Booth!" he cheered. "Congrats!"

I had never won anything in my life. Putting the bracelet on, I felt my luck start to change. I felt taller and cooler! I even stepped on a banana peel . . . and didn't slip!

"Woo!" Regina cheered. "You really know how to *claw* your way to the top!"

"Speech! Speech! Speech!" Mr. Hughes said.

I tried to say something about how awesome my booth had turned out, but then I had a slow realization. Even though I'd just won the bracelet, I had already felt lucky way before then. I'd felt it the moment I'd met my friends!

"I think we're all winners here," I said. "And we *all* deserve a bit of this prize."

Glinda sighed. "I sense this is going to be a very cheesy moment."

"I love cheese," Jake whispered.

I tried slipping the bracelet off, and you'll never believe what happened. It broke. The chain snapped apart and the four-leaf-clover charm flew right off!

"Well," Glinda deadpanned. "So much for luck."

Regina laughed. "Should we try the Ferris wheel before it shuts down?"

"Yes, yes, yes!" Jake sprinted off.

"Here." Glinda handed me the four-leaf-clover charm. "If we're all getting on that thing with you, let's at least pretend nothing will go wrong."

If the good luck had disappeared from the bracelet, I couldn't tell. I was too busy laughing and having fun with my friends.

Have you ever had one of those days where you wake up and everything is just right?

Usually, my days are a messy blur of running late, spilling sticky breakfast all over myself, or accidentally wearing two different shoes.

But today? It was nothing like that.

An excerpt from *Catch Zoo Later*

Today, I arrived at school *extra* early. I was extra excited. Everything was *extra* perfect. This was because today was ... FIELD TRIP DAY!

It was like the weekend traded places with a weekday, bringing my friends along for the fun!

Outside the school building, my class gathered at the school's bus zone. Kids chatted excitedly, dressed in their field-trip best.

Jake Gold, all-star athlete and all-star best friend, was doing something strange with his knees. This was called "exercising."

An excerpt from *Catch Zoo Later*

Another of my friends, Regina du Lar, coached him with her tablet. She tapped it and a sound came out like a coach's whistle. *FWEEET*!

"Time out!" she shouted, then smiled at me. "Look, Jake, ▆▆▆▆▆▆▆ is here!"

"Ninety-eight . . . ninety-nine . . . one hundred!" Jake counted out loud. He paused his jumping jacks and smiled. "Hey, bro! Don't mind me. I'm just prepping to be the fastest thing at the zoo today."

That's where we were going today— the zoo!

An excerpt from *Catch Zoo Later*